The Great Halloween Costume Contest

By Lauren Turnowski
Illustrated by Mindy M. Pierce

Grosset & Dunlap • New York

Library of Congress Control Number: 2003103344

ISBN 0-448-43115-7   BCDEFGHIJ

It's Halloween.
All the kids in town are getting ready for the big costume party.

On Candy Corn Lane,
Sally blows up big green balloons for her costume.

On Spooky Street,
Jack puts yellow tape "stripes" on his black T-shirt.

In the orange house on Pumpkin Way,
Stacy and Tracy decorate for the big party.

(Use the pom-poms to help them decorate their house.)

Soon it is nighttime.
The kids are ready to leave for the party.

First there are games to play.
The kids bob for apples.
Look at the piñata!
Stacy gets ready to knock it down.

Time to eat!
Everyone gets to decorate a cupcake.

Soon it is time for the costume contest.
The kids are so excited!

Sally marches to the front of the room,
covered in big green balloons.
What could she be?
A bunch of juicy grapes!

Here comes Jack.
When he shakes his head, his black antennae bop up and down.
Can you guess what he is?
That's easy! He's a buzzing bumblebee!

Lilly and Sam come up together.
Sam's silver costume is shiny with
red lights that blink on and off.

Lilly's big purple feet and hands flop all around.
Two aliens in their spaceships have landed at
the party!

The rest of the kids show off their costumes one by one.
There's a clown and a dinosaur and a lion that roars,
a pretty pink princess and a giant that snores.

Now the contest is over.
Everybody's costume looks great.
Who will take home first prize?
It's so hard to decide.

But wait!
Someone is at the door.

It's Zippy the dog!
He's wearing a costume, too!
Zippy has come dressed as a yummy hot dog.

Everyone laughs and cheers.
The winner has been chosen.
Stacy and Tracy place the first-prize medal around Zippy's neck.
The Halloween costume contest is over—until next year!

There are lots of fun things to do with pom-poms! Follow the instructions to make your very own Halloween crafts. Make sure to cover the space where you are working with old newspapers and always wear a smock to protect your clothing. Remember to ask an adult for permission before starting any of these projects. Have fun!

Handprint ghosts

What you'll need:

Washable white paint
Small paintbrush
Black construction paper
Pom-pom stickers

1. Using a small paintbrush, paint the palm of one of your hands with the white paint.
2. Make a palm print on the black construction paper
3. Turn the paper upside down—now you have a spooky ghost!
4. Use the pom-poms to decorate your ghostly friends.
5. Make sure to wash your hands after you are done!

Trick-or-treat bags

What you'll need:

Large brown paper bags with handles (available at craft stores or your local supermarket)
Different colored paints (Halloween colors, of course!)
Paintbrushes
Pom-pom stickers

1. Use the paint to decorate your paper bag with spooky Halloween designs.
2. When the paint dries, create some more Halloween fun with the sparkly pom-poms.
3. Use your new trick-or-treat bag to collect some yummy Halloween goodies!

Picture frames

What you'll need:

Colored cardstock (preferably in Halloween colors)
Pom-pom stickers
Scissors   Tape
Pencil   Ruler
Glue   Markers

1. Using the ruler and a pencil, draw a rectangle in the middle of a piece of cardstock. The rectangle should be 8 inches long on one side and 5 inches long on the other.
2. Have an adult help you cut the rectangle out of the cardstock.
3. Use the pom-poms to decorate your frame. You can also use the markers to draw spooky Halloween designs or use the leftover cardstock to cut out Halloween figures and glue them to the frame.
4. Take your favorite Halloween photo and tape it to the back of the frame so that the picture shows through the cut-out space. Now you have a BOO-tiful frame in which to display you in your Halloween costume!